The Scared Little Rabbit

written by Dalton Atchley

AuthorHouse™
1663 Liberty Drive
Bloomington, IN 47403
www.authorhouse.com
Phone: 1 (800) 839-8640

This book is printed on acid-free paper.

ISBN: 978-1-7283-3106-5 (sc)
ISBN: 978-1-7283-3107-2 (e)

Print information available on the last page.

Published by AuthorHouse 10/10/2019

authorHOUSE®

The Scared Little Rabbit

written by Dalton Atchley

Once there lived a little rabbit named Hector. Hector lived with his parents in a small burrow deep in the woods. The burrow was made up of sticks and grass and had two rooms. Now, Hector was not the bravest little rabbit in the world. Hector was scared of a great many things, such as thunder storms, snakes, spiders and even worms.

One night a big thunderstorm came through the woods and Hector couldn't sleep at all because he was so scared. Hector ran to his parents' room and hid under their bed. Hector's mom and dad had told Hector that there was no reason for him to be scared of those things. But there was no telling Hector not to be scared.

The next morning, poor, tired Hector went out to search the woods for berries that they would eat for breakfast. Once he found the berries, Hector's mom said, "Eat up. Breakfast is the most important meal of the day."

So, hungry, Hector started gobbling down his breakfast, but as he was eating, he looked up to see a snake slithering his way. "Ahh!" Hector screamed, running to hide behind his mom. "It's okay, dear," Hector's mom said to him.

But once again, Hector didn't listen. He was still very much scared. Hector vowed never to return to the berry patch again. On his way back home, Hector felt something crawling on his leg. Hector looked down and saw a big black spider. Hector was so scared the he hopped five feet into the air, screamed and ran away.

Later that day, Hector, his mom and his dad returned home. Hector slowly walked inside to take his nap. But when he got to his bed, he saw a worm crawling slowly past the bed.

But before he could turn tail and run away screaming, the worm looked at him and said, "Hey, I've heard of you." "You have?" Hector asked. "Yeah you are that little rabbit that's scared of everything." "Hey, you have heard of me." Hector said surprised.

"But listen to me kid." The worm said. "I've been around a while, and one thing that I have learned is that all animals feel fear." "They do?" Hector asked. "Of course, they do." Said the worm. Shocked Hector asked. "Even the scary ones?"

"Of course." The worm said back to Hector. "You know that snake you saw today?" "Yeah." Said Hector. "When you got scared and screamed, he slithered off because he was scared too." Said the worm. "Well, I better get going or I'll be late for dinner."

The worm slowly crawled off. It was at that moment in his life that Hector finally realized that there is really nothing to be scared of.

Printed in the United States
By Bookmasters